Pride comes before a fall

Honesty is the best policy

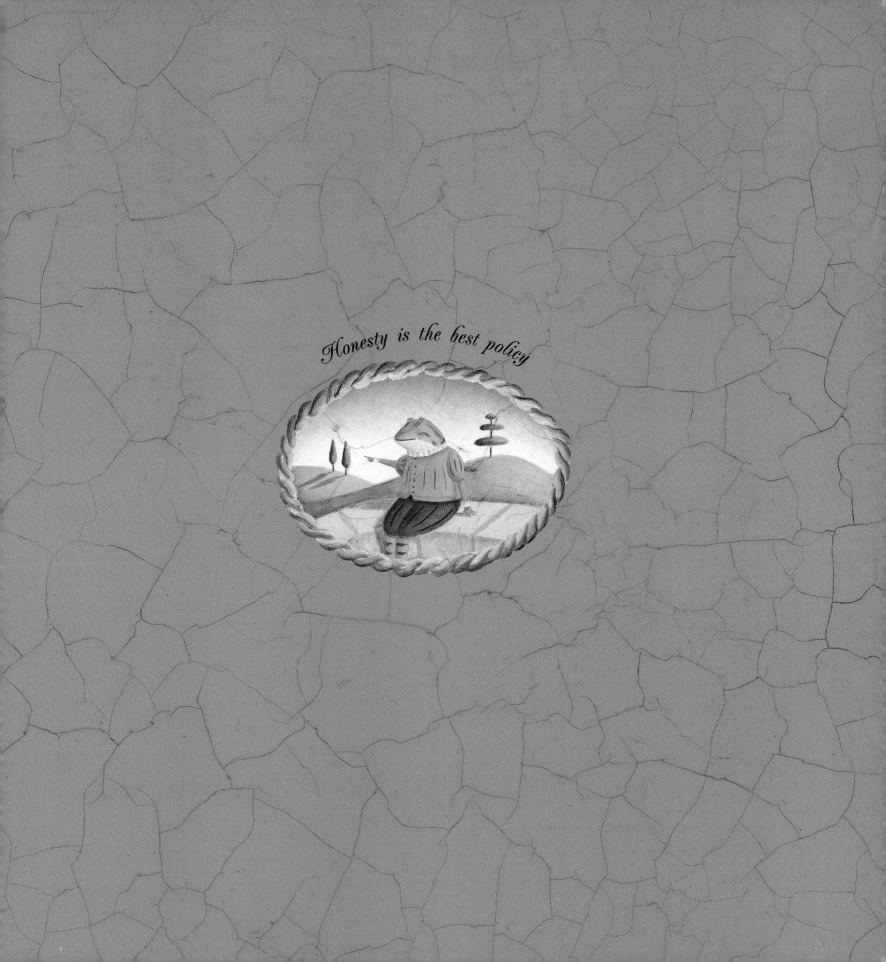

A TEMPLAR BOOK
First published in the UK in 2004 by Templar Publishing.
This softback edition published in the UK in 2015 by Templar Publishing,
an imprint of The Templar Company Limited,
Deepdene Lodge, Deepdene Avenue, Dorking, Surrey, RH5 4AT
www.templarco.co.uk

Illustration copyright © 2004 by Alison Jay
Text and design copyright © 2004 by The Templar Company Limited

1 3 5 7 9 10 8 6 4 2

ISBN 978-1-78370-146-9

Designed by janie louise hunt
Edited by A.J. Wood & Sue Harris

Printed in China

THE EMPEROR'S
NEW CLOTHES

Retold by Marcus Sedgwick

Illustrated by Alison Jay

templar publishing

One day the Emperor got out of bed
and slowly scratched his sleepy head.
"Something's wrong, and I know what!
My subjects do not care a jot
for who I am and what I do.
They show no gratitude, it's true!"
"What I badly need," he said,
"is something to make my people see
that they should be proud of a King like me,
that I am worthy of respect.
That's surely not much to expect!"

As if by magic, the very next day,
there came a knock on the palace door.
Two young weasels stood on the step:
"We're just what the
Emperor's looking for!"
"We are tailors," the weasels said,
"the finest tailors in all the land!
We can weave you clothes so grand
that all your people
will stop and stand
and stare and say, 'Why, goodness me!
There is no Emperor quite like he!'"
"Just the thing!"
the Emperor said.

"But that's not all!" the tailors cried.
"There's something more.
For we spin spells as well as wool,
to make cloth that's invisible to all who dull or foolish be.
Our magic clothes they cannot see!
Just a little more gold will secure such a spell.
We're sure it will serve you remarkably well!"
The King was delighted.

"Splendid, splendid! Start straight away!
Arrange a grand procession day!
I'll wear the clothes which you have made
and my subjects will cheer as I parade!"

"But can we afford it?" the tortoise cried,
the doors of the treasury open wide.
Hare agreed, and dared to state,
"We have already spent far too much
on trousers and suits and hats and such!"
"Balderdash!" the Emperor cried.
"Such a suit will let me see
those who wise or foolish be—
those unfit for the office they hold!
Chamberlain! Do as you're told!"

But the Emperor had made an awful mistake.
The weasels weren't tailors at all, they were fake.
And when Hare left them to start their work,
the two young rascals began to smirk.
Smiling and joking, and giggling and more,
they laughed and rolled upon the floor.
"I never thought we'd fool them so well.
Who would have thought
they'd believe in a spell!"

"How easily people are taken in,
taken in by a tale so thin!"
"But the tale's a good one, woven with care.
It's only the cloth that isn't there!"

(And Hare,
listening at the door,
wondered what all
the **laughter** was for...)

Many days passed, without a sign
of any clothes, either shabby or fine.
And the poor old Emperor began to doubt
that he'd ever get his parade shoes out!
"It's time I saw these wonderful clothes,"
moaned the Emperor,
grumpily scratching his nose.
"But suppose, when I visit, I can't see a thing.
Then I'd look like a fool
and I am the King!
I don't want to seem like a dunderhead!
I'll send my servants to look instead!"

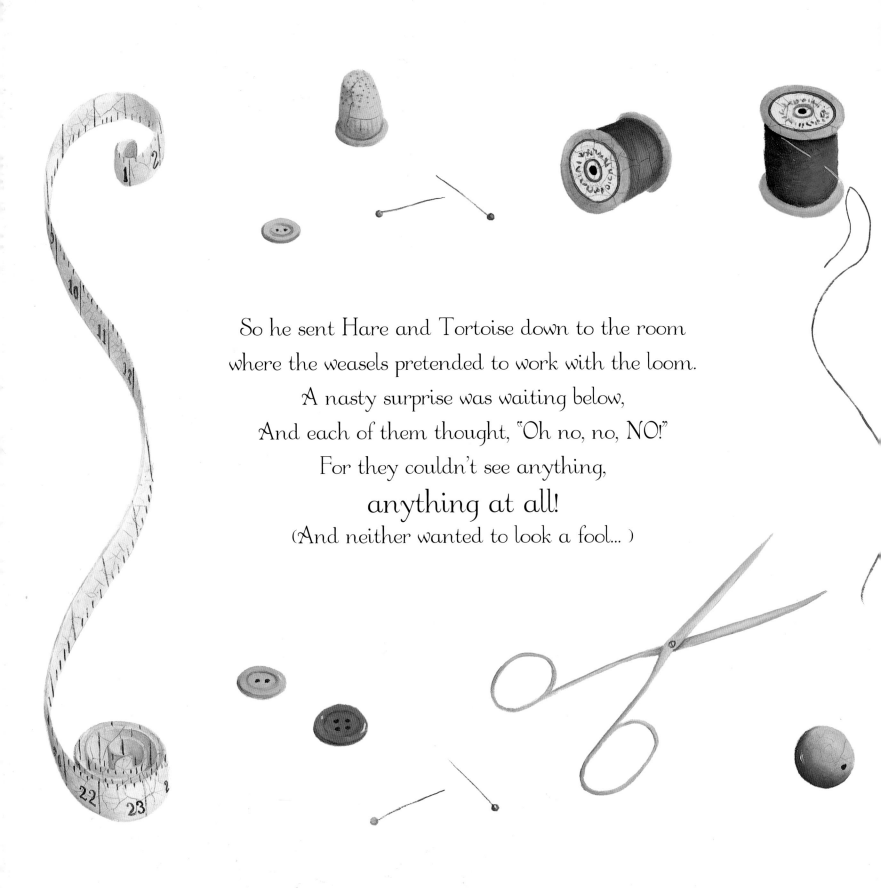

So he sent Hare and Tortoise down to the room
where the weasels pretended to work with the loom.
A nasty surprise was waiting below,
And each of them thought, "Oh no, no, NO!"
For they couldn't see anything,
anything at all!
(And neither wanted to look a fool...)

By now the Emperor was eager to know
what had become of his fabulous clothes.
"Tell me!" he cried to Tortoise and Hare,
of the clothes they'd not seen,
the clothes that weren't there.
"What are they like?

Are they sumptuous and rich? Are they beautifully stitched?
Are they **special** and **super** and **lovely** and **fine**?
Are they MINE?"

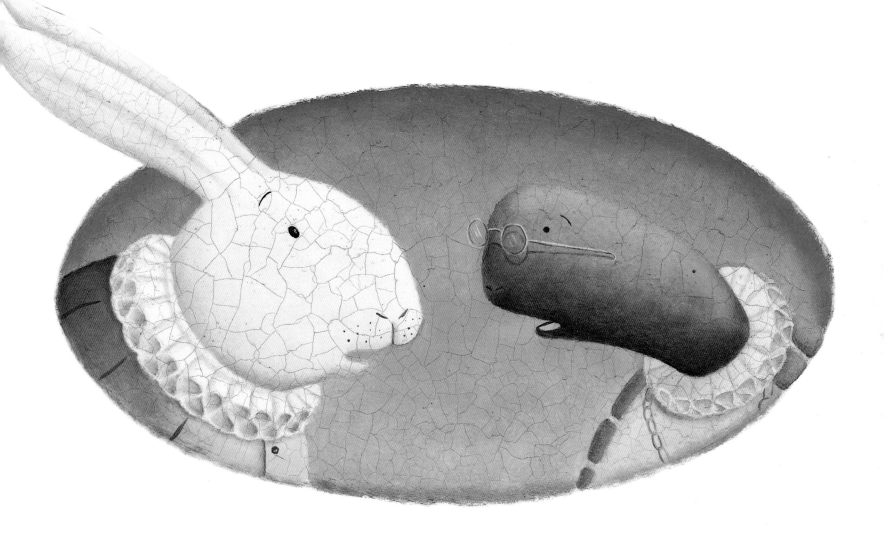

Hare and Tortoise looked for somewhere to hide.
"They look wonderful!" they lied.

The day of the procession
at last had come,
eagerly awaited by everyone.
The weasels fussed
and **patted** and **preened**.
Slyly, they told him,
"They fit like a dream!"
And the Emperor pretended not to care
that he seemed to be
dressed in clothes **that**
weren't there.

The procession set out from the palace gates
and everyone stared and gazed and gawped,
too frightened to say what they
really thought.

But then came a voice; a small frog's cry,
who shouted, "Look!" after wondering why,
the Emperor was bare!
He wasn't impressed
that the foolish old lion wasn't properly dressed.
After that, the secret was out!
And everyone started to point and shout
and laugh and make a hullabaloo.
For the trick was exposed,
and the Emperor too!

Beware of false flattery

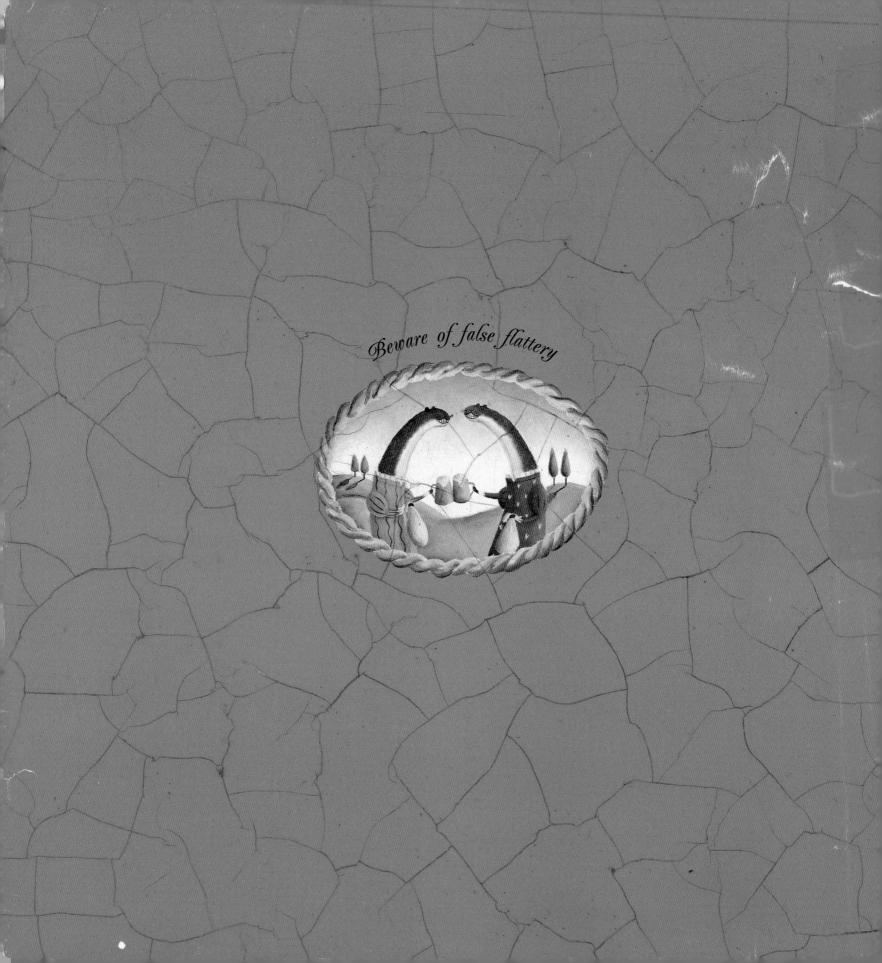

A fool and his money are soon parted